29300

APR 1 3 2005   FEB 2 1 2008

JUN 0 8 2005   MAR 2 2 2008

JUL 0 9 2005   MAR 2 8 2008

AUG 3 1 2005   JUN 0 3 2008

FEB 1 7 2006   NOV 0 7 2008

MAR 1 4 2006   APR 0 9 2014

JUL 2 0 2006

SEP 1 4 2006

NOV 0 4 2006

MAR 0 9 2007

JUL 2 6 2007

OCT 0 3 2007

NOV 0 2 2007

DEC 1 9 2007

JAN 2 3 2008

How To Draw Garfield & the Gang

BY JIM DAVIS

A CREATIVE MEDIA APPLICATIONS PRODUCTION; FABIA WARGIN DESIGNS—DESIGN; ALAN BARNETT, INC.—PRODUCTION; RON ZALME—ILLUSTRATIONS; MICHAEL TEITELBAUM, RON ZALME, SCOTT NICKEL—TEXT

SCHOLASTIC INC.

**New York   Toronto   London   Auckland   Sydney
Mexico City   New Delhi   Hong Kong   Buenos Aires**

ISBN   0-439-63821-6

12 11 10 9 8 7 6 5 4 3 2 1   4 5 6 7 8/0

Printed in the U.S.A.   40

First Scholastic printing, December 2003

INTRODUCTION

HELLO, ART LOVERS AND FELINE FANCIERS! GARFIELD HERE.

They say there are those who are born great, those who achieve greatness, and those who have greatness thrust upon them. All three statements apply to me — plus I'm drawn great, too!

If you read my comic strip or watch my animated TV show (and you have to — it's the law!) and have always wanted to learn how to draw me, you've come to the right place. This book will take you step-by-step through the process of drawing cartoons. When you're finished, you'll be able to draw me in my many moods — hungry, sleepy, and hungry — in lots of different poses such as sleeping, snacking, napping, resting, eating, and occasionally even standing up.

You'll also learn how to draw the entire Garfield gang: Odie, my clueless canine sidekick; Jon, my geeky owner; Arlene, my feline gal pal; Nermal, the (ugh!) world's cutest kitten; and Pooky, my huggable teddy bear. Then, once you've practiced the basics, you can create your own comic strips. All you'll need is pencil, paper, and imagination (and a snack — drawing can work up an appetite!).

Although I consider myself a self-made cat, I do owe a little of my success to cartoonist Jim Davis. On June 19, 1978, cartooning history was changed forever. On that fateful day (isn't it a national holiday yet?), Jim unveiled his new comic strip entitled "Garfield." When Jim first started drawing my entertaining exploits, I appeared in only 41 newspapers, but today my lovable likeness brings laughs to readers of more than 2,500 papers worldwide!

But enough talk! Now it's time to pick up your pencils, grab a piece of paper, and make some cartoon magic. If you follow the simple instructions in this book, you'll be sketching like a pro in no time!

Well, all this excitement has worn me out. I need a big snack and a long nap!

— Garfield

GARFIELD'S HEAD

Hey, future cartoonists of the world! Before you begin drawing, here are a couple of quick tips:
1) Draw lightly as you sketch. You'll have plenty of time to darken your lines as you finish your drawing and fill in the details. 2) Stay loose (like a goose!). Let your hand and arm move freely. Don't tighten up or hold your pencil in a "death grip." Relax! Drawing, like eating, should be a fun activity. 3) Don't be

1. START WITH A BASIC OVAL SHAPE - LIKE A WATERMELON (YUM!). DRAW A STRAIGHT LINE DIVIDING THE OVAL IN HALF VERTICALLY. THEN DRAW A HORIZONTAL LINE 1/4 OF THE WAY UP FROM THE BOTTOM OF THE OVAL. CURVE THIS LINE SO IT APPEARS TO BE GOING AROUND THE OVAL.

2. DRAW A SMALL CIRCLE FOR GARFIELD'S NOSE RIGHT WHERE THE VERTICAL AND HORIZONTAL LINES CROSS. ADD EARS. THEN DRAW TWO LARGE OVALS FOR HIS EYES (ALSO KNOWN AS "PASTA SPOTTERS"). GIVE HIM A NICE BIG SMILE. THE ENDS OF THE SMILE SHOULD REACH HALFWAY UP HIS EYE OVALS.

3. COMPLETE THE EARS AND ADD ONE EXTRA LINE TO GIVE GARFIELD HIS FAMOUS DOUBLE CHIN. NOW ADD HIS WHISKERS, EYELIDS, AND TWO DOTS FOR HIS EYES.

4. CLEAN UP THE SKETCHY PENCIL LINES WITH AN ERASER AND ADD THE FINAL STRIPES AND DOTS AND - PRESTO!! — YOU'VE COMPLETED GARFIELD'S HEAD. BEHOLD THE HUNGRIEST CAT IN HISTORY!

afraid to make a mistake – that's why they invented erasers! 4) Finally, remember that the poses in this book are guides to help you understand how to draw me and my friends by building on basic shapes. The more you practice drawing, the better you'll get, and soon you'll be able to make up your own poses, situations, and stories (just make sure you draw lots of food for me to eat!).

1. JUST AS WITH THE FRONT VIEW, START WITH A LARGE OVAL AND ADD THE HORIZONTAL AND VERTICAL LINES, ONLY THIS TIME PLACE THE VERTICAL LINE OFF-CENTER (TOWARD THE SIDE YOU WANT GARFIELD TO FACE) AND CURVE THE LINE SO IT APPEARS TO BE GOING AROUND THE OVAL.

2. ADD THE EYE OVALS, EARS, NOSE, AND MOUTH AS BEFORE, ONLY THIS TIME NOTICE THAT THE EARS BOTH ANGLE TOWARD THE SIDE YOU WANT GARFIELD TO FACE.

3. FILL OUT GARFIELD'S FACE AND NOTE HOW THE CHIN AND CHEEK LINES OVERLAP IN THE SAME DIRECTION.

4. CLEAN UP THE SKETCHY PENCIL LINES WITH AN ERASER, AND ADD THE FINAL STRIPES AND DOTS. NOTICE THAT YOU SEE MORE STRIPES ON THE SIDE OF THE HEAD THAT'S TURNED TOWARD YOU.

Now that you've learned how to draw Garfield's head, let's give the feisty fat cat some facial expressions:
1) Keep ovals somewhat flattened on bottom. 2) Lips thicken at ends. 3) Note extra height of head for the happy and excited (in other words, hungry) look. Also, the teeth are evenly spaced squares extending out

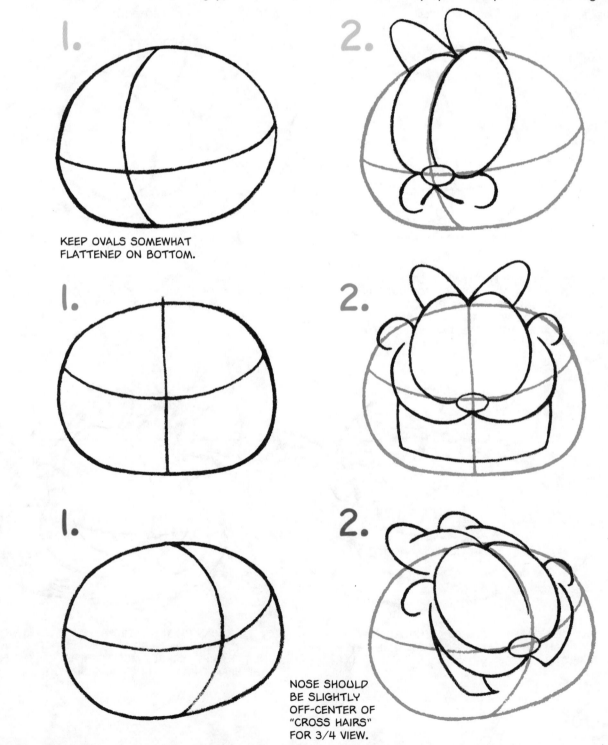

1.

KEEP OVALS SOMEWHAT
FLATTENED ON BOTTOM.

2.

1.

2.

1.

2.

NOSE SHOULD
BE SLIGHTLY
OFF-CENTER OF
"CROSS HAIRS"
FOR 3/4 VIEW.

from both sides of the center of the smile. 4) Nose should be slightly off-center of the crossing horizontal and vertical lines in the three-quarter views. 5) Ears and whiskers sweep back for a "speedy" look.

3. LIPS THICKEN AT ENDS.

4.

3. NOTE EXTRA HEIGHT OF HEAD FOR THAT HAPPY OR EXCITED LOOK.

TEETH ARE EVENLY SPACED SQUARES FROM CENTER OF SMILE.

4.

3. EARS AND WHISKERS SWEEP BACK FOR A "SPEEDY" LOOK.

4.

GARFIELD'S BODY

SITTING

1. TO SHOW GARFIELD'S ENTIRE BODY, START WITH TWO LARGE OVALS (AND LOTS OF PAPER)—ONE OVAL FOR HIS HEAD, ONE FOR HIS BODY. DIVIDE THE HEAD OVAL WITH HORIZONTAL AND VERTICAL LINES AS BEFORE. MAKE THE BODY OVAL FLAT ON THE BOTTOM.

2. PLACE CIRCLES ALONG THE BOTTOM LINE OF THE BODY OVAL TO POSITION THE FEET AND TAIL. ADD THE EYE OVALS, EARS, NOSE, AND MOUTH.

STANDING

1. AGAIN, USE TWO OVALS FOR THE HEAD AND BODY. GARFIELD'S TUBE-SHAPED LEGS ARE QUITE LONG WHEN HE'S STANDING. CENTER THEM UNDER THE BODY OVAL SO THEY LOOK BALANCED. THEN ADD HIS FEET AS SHOWN.

2. IT'S EASIER TO THINK OF GARFIELD'S HANDS AS ONE ENTIRE SHAPE WHEN SKETCHING, SO THE FINGERS DON'T GET OUT OF PROPORTION. DRAW THESE AS SHOWN, THEN ADD HIS TAIL.

3. FILL IN THE PAWS AND ROUND OUT THE BODY TO GIVE GARFIELD HIS FAMOUS PEAR SHAPE (ALTHOUGH HE GOT IT MORE FROM EATING FRIED FOOD THAN FROM FRUIT). FILL IN FACIAL DETAILS AS BEFORE.

4. CLEAN UP THE SKETCH LINES AND FINISH YOUR DRAWING BY ADDING GARFIELD'S STRIPES.

3. NOW IT'S TIME TO FILL IN THE DETAILS OF HIS FINGERS AND TOES. ALSO NOTICE HOW THE SHAPE OF HIS HEEL CHANGES.

4. DRAW THE FINAL DETAILS. DID YOU REMEMBER TO ADD THE SHADOWS AT THE TOP OF GARFIELD'S REAR LEG AND TAIL?

Now that you've learned how to draw Garfield's body, let's put him in some common poses:

SLEEPING

1.

SCRUNCH UP THE BODY OVAL TO GIVE GARFIELD A COZY LOOK WHILE HE'S SLEEPING.

2.

WALKING

1. WHEN HIS FEET, HANDS, OR TAIL GO BEHIND HIS BODY, IT GIVES YOUR DRAWING A 3-D FEELING.

2.

A SMOOTH CURVE TO THE TAIL GIVES THE FAT CAT THE LOOK OF LIVELY ACTION.

RUNNING

1.

2.

3.

3.

3.

THE TINIER THE
EYES, THE MORE
GARFIELD WILL
LOOK FRIGHTENED
OR SURPRISED.

TRY
THESE:

FRONT VIEW

1. TO DRAW A FRONT VIEW, START WITH A CIRCLE. THEN DIVIDE IT WITH HORIZONTAL AND VERTICAL LINES AS SHOWN.

2. CENTER THE NOSE, ADD THE EYES AND EARS, AND CHANGE THE FACE SHAPE AS SHOWN. NOTE HOW THE CHEEKS LINE UP ON THE HORIZONTAL LINE.

3. ODIE'S EARS SHOULD BE PERKY. THE OVAL SHAPES AT THE END OF HIS EARS HELP GIVE THEM VOLUME AND WEIGHT. ADD THE FINAL DETAILS AS WELL AS THE HIGHLIGHT ON ODIE'S NOSE.

4. CLEAN UP YOUR ORIGINAL OVAL, AND THE HORIZONTAL AND VERTICAL LINES. THEN FILL IN THE NOSE AND THE NECK SHADOW, AND YOU'RE DONE!

EXPRESSIONS

SIDE VIEW

1. TO DRAW A SIDE VIEW, CONNECT TWO OVALS FOR THE HEAD AND THE MUZZLE. THEN DRAW TWO LINES FOR THE NECK.

1. DRAW THE ENTIRE NECK SHAPE IN YOUR SKETCH, THEN ADD THE MOUTH AND TONGUE (WATCH OUT FOR DOG BREATH!).

2.

3.

2.

3.

13

1. DRAW ODIE STANDING USING OVALS, CYLINDERS (FOR HIS NECK AND LEGS), AND HALF-CIRCLES FOR HIS FEET. THE DOTTED LINES ARE THERE IN THE SKETCH JUST TO SHOW YOU HOW THE SHAPES SHOULD FIT INTO ONE ANOTHER. THE LINES SHOULD NOT APPEAR IN YOUR DRAWING.

2. ADD THE EARS, BRING UP THE MUZZLE LINE FOR A GREAT BIG SMILE, AND THEN ADD THE MOUTH TO THE NECK SHAPE.

3. ADD DETAILS, INCLUDING THE TAIL, THE TONGUE (DROOL IS OPTIONAL), THE HAIRS ON THE BACK OF HIS HEAD, AND THE SPOT ON HIS SIDE.

4. CLEAN UP THE SKETCH LINES WITH AN ERASER. THEN FILL IN THE BLACK AREAS AND SHADOWS.

POSITIONS

1. ODIE'S REAR LEGS LOSE THEIR TUBE SHAPE WHEN THEY ARE DRAWN UP CLOSE TO HIS BODY.

2. SWEEP THE EARS AND TONGUE BACK TO ADD THE APPEARANCE OF SPEED AND MOVEMENT TO THE DRAWING.

1. STRETCH OUT ODIE'S BODY TO MAKE HIM LOOK RELAXED.

2.

1. USE THE SAME OVAL FOR ODIE'S BODY AS IN THE SIDE VIEW, BUT THIS TIME IT SHOULD BE DRAWN BEHIND HIS NECK.

2.

3.

JON

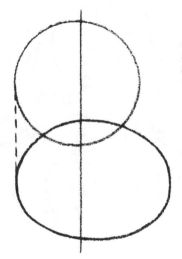

1. START BY STACKING A CIRCLE OVER AN OVAL, BUT DON'T CENTER THEM. THE DOTTED LINE SHOWS HOW TO LINE UP THESE SHAPES WHERE THEY BECOME THE BACK OF JON'S HEAD.

2. ADD JON'S EYES AND MOUTH AS SHOWN. THE STRAIGHT LINE DOWN THE MIDDLE IS THERE TO HELP YOU LINE UP HIS EYES, HIS NECK, AND THE TOP OF HIS HEAD.

3. JON'S HAIR IS ALWAYS MADE UP OF THE SAME AMOUNT OF BUMPS. IT WILL TAKE SOME PRACTICE TO GET THEM TO FLOW OVER THE TOP OF HIS HEAD CORRECTLY, AS SHOWN HERE.

4. FINISH YOUR DRAWING BY ADDING A FEW STRAY HAIRS AND THEN FILL IN THE SHADOWS.

1. USE AN OVAL TO GIVE JON HIS POTBELLIED SLOUCH.

2.

3. USE A WHITE LINE TO SEPARATE JON'S TWO BLACK LEGS.

1. TILT THE HEAD SHAPES TO GIVE HIM THE IMPRESSION OF ACTION AND MOVEMENT.

2. DRAW JON'S LEGS TO FIT INSIDE HIS PANTS.

ARLENE

1. JUST LIKE GARFIELD, ARLENE'S HEAD STARTS WITH AN OVAL AND HORIZONTAL AND VERTICAL GUIDELINES.

2. ADD HER NOSE, EYES, EARS, AND A CURVED LINE AT THE BOTTOM OF THE OVAL FOR HER SMILE.

3. GIVE ARLENE'S HEAD A LITTLE EXTRA HEIGHT BY EXTENDING THE SIDES OF THE OVAL UP TO HER EARS. USE ANOTHER OVAL TO CREATE HER LOWER LIP.

4. FINISH HER EARS JUST LIKE GARFIELD'S AND THEN ADD ARLENE'S EYELASHES.

WATCH OUT, SUPERMODELS!

1. THE OVAL FOR ARLENE'S BODY IS ROUGHLY HALFWAY BETWEEN HER HEAD AND FEET.

2. TUCK IN THE OVAL AT HER BACK SO SHE IS NOT TOO ROUND.

3.

1.

2.

3. THE FINGERS ARE MADE FROM SMALL OVALS.

LOOK AT YOUR OWN HANDS IN A MIRROR. WHAT SHAPES WOULD YOU USE TO DRAW THEM?

POOKY

1. START WITH YOUR BASIC OVAL, BUT KEEP IT FLATTENED ON THE BOTTOM AS SHOWN. DRAW YOUR HORIZONTAL AND VERTICAL GUIDELINES.

2. ADD TWO DOUBLE CIRCLES TO THE TOP OF THE OVAL (THEY LOOK LIKE DOUGHNUTS, DON'T THEY?) FOR POOKY'S EARS. LEAVE SOME SPACE BETWEEN THE EARS. THE TOP OF HIS HEAD WILL GO BETWEEN THEM.

3. EXTEND THE TOP OF HIS HEAD AND HIS "HAIR." DRAW NOTCHES TO THE TOPS OF HIS EARS IN THE SHAPE OF BACKWARDS Z'S.

4. COMPLETE YOUR DRAWING OF POOKY AS SHOWN. THE LINES AT THE BOTTOM OF HIS FACE SHOULDN'T ACTUALLY TOUCH.

1. POOKY IS A STUFFED TOY, SO HE DOESN'T MOVE BY HIMSELF. KEEP THAT IN MIND WHILE YOU ARE DRAWING HIM.

2. ADD SHADOWS AS SHOWN TO GIVE THE FIGURE SHAPE AND VOLUME.

NERMAL

1. ONCE AGAIN, BEGIN BY DRAWING THE OVAL AND ADD LINES THAT FORM THE FRAMEWORK FOR THE HEAD.

2. POSITION NERMAL'S NOSE, EYES, EARS, AND BIG SMILE AS SHOWN.

3. NOTICE THE DIFFERENCE BETWEEN NERMAL'S EARS AND THOSE OF GARFIELD AND ARLENE.

4. THE STRIPES AND EYELASHES ARE WHAT GIVE NERMAL HIS "WORLD'S CUTEST KITTEN" LOOK. ADD THEM LAST TO COMPLETE YOUR DRAWING.

1.

NERMAL'S LEGS
ARE NOT AS LONG
AS GARFIELD'S.

2.

3.

NERMAL'S EXPRESSION IS ALMOST ALWAYS
BRIGHT AND CHEERFUL (WHICH IS ONE OF
THE REASONS WHY GARFIELD HATES HIM!).

1.

NOTICE THAT NERMAL'S
LEG DOESN'T GET
LONGER, BUT BEING ON
HIS TOES DOES GIVE HIM
EXTRA HEIGHT.

2.

BE CAREFUL NOT TO MIX
UP THE OVERLAP OF ARM,
EAR, TAIL, AND LEG, OR YOU
WILL FLATTEN OUT THE
3-D EFFECT.

OTHER CHARACTERS

Here are some kooky characters to try your hand at!

> SHOW ME A GOOD MOUSER, AND I'LL SHOW YOU A CAT WITH BAD BREATH!

GARFIELD AND SQUEAK THE MOUSE

JON'S DAD

JON'S MOM

JON'S BROTHER DOC BOY

LIZ THE VETERINARIAN

BINKY THE CLOWN

TWANG! SMACK!

© 1995 PAWS, INC. Distributed by Universal Press Syndicate

JIM DAVIS 11-28

GARFIELD SAYS THAT A DAY WITHOUT SPIDER-WHACKING IS LIKE A DAY WITHOUT PASTA.

A FEW OF THE FAT CAT'S FAVORITE THINGS: A JOLTING CUP OF JAVA, A WARM BED, A FAST REMOTE CONTROL, AND A FULL FOOD DISH.

GARFI

CLICK CLICK CLICK
CLICK CLICK CLICK C
CLICK CLICK CLICK CLIC
K CLICK CLICK CLI
CLICK CLICK
CK CLI
CLICK CLI
CK CLICK CLI
CK CLICK
CLICK CLI

TAPPITY

TAPPITY
TAPPITY

EFFECTS & STUFF

The Garfield comic strip appears in more than 2,500 newspapers around the world, making it one of the most widely read strips ever! Day in and day out, Jim Davis keeps readers laughing with the wacky adventures of Garfield, Jon, Odie, and the gang. Let's take a behind-the-scenes look at how this popular daily comic is created.

THE ROUGH SKETCH

Every Garfield comic strip begins with a rough sketch. This quick pencil drawing shows the characters' expressions, what they are doing, and where they should be placed within the comic strip panel. The rough sketch also includes any editorial copy for the strip.

THE BLUE-LINE DRAWING

Using the rough sketch as a guide, the strip is then drawn in blue pencil. Blue pencil is used because the blue line will not show up on film when the final, inked version of the strip is photographed for printing in the newspaper. At this stage, the characters are drawn completely, and scenery or background details are added.

INKING THE STRIP

In the final step, a brush is used to trace a black line over the blue pencil line. The editorial copy is also inked in. Then Jim Davis signs and dates the strip, and it is ready to appear in the newspaper... but, not until weeks — or even months — later! Cartoonists have to work ahead!

Sunday may be the day of rest, but for Garfield it's also the day of jest, and in this larger format, the fat cat can really cut loose and go crazy with more mirth, madness, and mayhem!

The Sunday strips are formatted so that they can be run by newspapers horizontally or vertically. These strips take longer to produce, so they must be created even earlier than the daily strips.

DROP PANEL
Depending on the way the strip is run, newspapers have the option of omitting this panel, so it is usually a "throwaway" gag or action panel that isn't essential to the strip.

LOGO BOX
Every week a fun new logo box is created around Garfield's name.

Because space in newspapers is limited, the Sunday strips have been designed so that the logo and drop panel can be left out without affecting the content of the comic.

Just as in the daily strips, a rough sketch is created, followed by a blue-line drawing, and then the final inking and lettering.

Next, the Sunday strip is "colored." After the strip is inked, a copy is made of the final art. Then, a color guide is created. The art is colored with markers and the colors are assigned numbers. This guide is sent to a company that colors the strip mechanically, and creates the four-color art that will appear in the newspapers.

Finally, the printed Garfield comic arrives to millions of readers on Sunday morning, just in time for breakfast (do I smell bacon?).

GARFIELD & THE GANG